MARIKO AND THE MAGIC MIRROR

Kristi Shimada

Mariko and the Magic Mirror

Copyright © 2019 Kristi Shimada.

Illustrations by Eko Setiawan.

www.kristishimada.com

DEDICATION

To my beautiful grandchildren Ryan, Scarlet,

Alana, Harrison, Aria, Jackson, Olivia, and Alivia.

Love you all, Grams

August 26, 2019

CHAPTER 1

Mariko sits next to her mother on her futon bed. Her silky black hair hangs below her shoulders. She is wearing her favorite fuchsia kimono with hand-painted white peonies. Her mother made it for her eighth birthday. It looks beautiful against her fair skin.

Mariko was sad that her mother's beautiful long black hair was once gone. After a few months of chemotherapy and radiation treatments her mother's hair is growing back. She was diagnosed with terminal cancer six months ago. In the past few weeks the cancer has spread throughout her body. The doctors have discontinued the treatments because it's not helping. Mariko's mother is now in hospice care. She wants to be able to be with her family when she passes on.

Mariko notices her mother's hands shake as she holds an old rosewood box. Her mother unties the red velvet ribbon and takes off the lid. She hands the box to Mariko.

"What is it, Mommy?"

"This box has been passed down through many generations. Your grandmother gave this to me on my eighth birthday. It's very special. Now it's yours, Mariko. It's time for you to learn about the magic within you like I did."

"What do you mean by magic within, Mommy?"

"That's for you to explore and find on your own."

Mariko looks inside the box. There is a beautiful red lacquered mirror inlayed with pink cherry blossoms made from rose quartz. Mariko runs her fingers across the back of the mirror.

"Mommy, it's so pretty. I will take good care of the mirror."

"Yes Mariko, it is very beautiful. The cherry blossoms represent love, beauty, and magic."

Her mother touches the mirror and smiles. Mariko wraps her arms around her mother and kisses her.

"I am going to show Daddy."

Mariko runs outside into the Japanese tea garden her father designed and built. There are maple, pine, and cherry blossom trees all manicured to precision.

Mariko loves the roses, peonies, and irises that are planted around the garden.

There is a cascading waterfall that flows into a koi pond. The sound is soothing and peaceful. Sometimes Mariko sleeps underneath the stars in the garden with her mother and father.

"Daddy, look what Mommy gave me." Her father pauses from raking the leaves around the pond and kneels to see.

"Mariko, your Mommy loves that mirror. She calls it her magic mirror."

"It's magic?"

She wonders how her father knows about the magic? Did her mother tell him about it? That's the only way he would know.

"Yes, you will see the magic come alive."

"Toshi, please hurry," Mariko can hear her mother's faint voice.

He drops his rake and runs inside. Mariko follows.

"Tomiko, what is it?" he asks.

She closes her eyes and whispers, "It's time, Toshi. I can see the flowers on the other side of the river."

Toshi holds her in his arms and tears flow down his cheeks.

Mariko looks at her father, and then her mother. She doesn't know what to think.

"I love you both so much. Please take care of each other. I will always be here in your hearts," whispers Tomiko.

"Daddy, what is happening? Mommy, please open your eyes." Her mother's body goes limp and she doesn't respond.

Mariko's father puts his arms around her and says, "Mariko, Mommy has passed to the other side of the river. Remember? We talked about this."

"Yes, I know but I am so sad." Mariko's tears stream down her face. She wiggles out of her father's arms and sits on the bed next to her mother. "Mommy, please don't go. Please don't leave us."

CHAPTER 2

Everyone is crying and praying as Reverend Sato reads from the Scriptures. The musician starts to play *My Eternal Light* on the harp. Mariko and her father are the first to place white roses and lilies on her mother's grave.

"Daddy, can Mommy hear us?" Mariko asks.

"Yes, she can hear us," he answers. Mariko feels comfort from her father's words.

"I love you, Mommy. I miss you." Mariko wipes the tears from her cheeks.

"It's time to go home, Mariko. We have guests coming over to celebrate your Mommy's life."

"Celebrate her life? She is not here to celebrate with us."

Mariko is confused.

"We are celebrating her life. Everyone wants to show their love and respect to your Mommy. We are mourning her death but celebrating her life that she shared with all of us," her father says.

CHAPTER 3

The drive home is silent. Mariko is happy to be home. When the car stops, she swings open the car door and runs to the teahouse. She stands in front of her wooden treasure chest. She throws back the heart- shaped latch and takes out her mirror.

Mariko sits on her favorite dreaming stone next to the koi pond. She can feel the warmth of the sun on her face. It makes her sleepy.

Mariko looks in the mirror and sees a reflection of an owl sitting on the old Japanese maple tree. She turns away from the mirror, looks back for the owl, but he is gone. When she looks into the mirror again, the white owl reappears. She closes her eyes and is scared to open them again. She feels herself falling.

CHAPTER 4

"What is happening?"

She opens her eyes and finds herself floating down a river in a small wooden rowboat. She is lying on top of soft rainbow-colored pillows. She feels cozy and safe. The scent of lilies reminds Mariko of her mother.

The vibrant colors of the flowers and trees are stunning. There are deer grazing near the river bed and birds flying from tree to tree. The grass is like emeralds glistening in the sun.

"Where am I?"

The owl she saw earlier flies down and sits at the edge of the boat.

"You are in a magical place where all things are possible. You have crossed the Rainbow Bridge," says the owl.

"Who are you?" Mariko asks.

"I am the great white owl of the rainbow bridge. My name is Niji. Do not be afraid. I will protect you. I used to take care of your mommy when she came to visit."

"You used to take care of my mommy? How can an owl take care of my mommy?"

Mariko looks around for the Rainbow Bridge. She doesn't remember crossing a bridge.

"Niji, what is the Rainbow Bridge?"

"The Rainbow Bridge takes you to the other side of the river. It is a bridge between realms. Just look in the mirror to find me. I am your guide. This is where all things are possible."

The rowboat lands on the shore of the Rainbow River where a white wolf is drinking water. The wolf turns and stares into Mariko's eyes. The wolf's blue eyes are like sparkling sapphires. Her fur is pure white.

"She is so beautiful," Mariko says.

Mariko can't stop looking at the wolf. She is drawn to her.

"Hello, Tomiko," Niji bows his head to the white wolf.

"Hello. I am happy to see you, Niji."

Tomiko looks at Mariko. "Mariko, I am happy you are visiting."

"Mommy, is that you? Why do you look like a wolf?"

"When you use the magic mirror it opens your eyes to all possibilities. I am still your mother."

"Are we in heaven?"

"No, we are not in heaven. You are visiting from earth and I am visiting from heaven. It's the space between the two. Your spirit travels through the mirror to different realms. The magic mirror guides you to new experiences and places. With the mirror you can come visit me at any time here in Rainbow Valley. I am always here."

Tomiko puts her paw on Mariko's heart. Mariko looks down at her reflection in the river. She looks the same as she does on earth.

"When I come to visit can I be an animal too?" Mariko asks.

"Yes, you can. Every person has an animal spirit that lives within. When I come to visit the Rainbow Valley, I become a white wolf. You have an animal spirit too. If you look inside yourself you will find your animal spirit. I will help you."

Tomiko trots up the riverbank.

CHAPTER 5

"Come, follow me. I will bring you to the *Spring of Knowing.* This is where you can see your spirit animal come to life," Tomiko says.

Mariko steps out of the boat and runs up the riverbank.

"Mommy, please wait. I can't run as fast as you trot."

Mariko tries to keep up. Tomiko slows down and waits. Mariko grabs onto her mother's tail and follows her into the forest. She looks up at the blue sky. The sun's rays light up the dirt path. A few feet in front of Mariko there is a beautiful waterfall flowing into an aquamarine pond from above.

"This is the Spring of Knowing. I want you to sit on the large rock in the center of the pond. Don't be afraid Mariko. The water is very shallow on this side."

Mariko steps into the pond. She stumbles on the slippery stones beneath her feet. She climbs up and notices that there is a pillow and a blanket on the large rock. The cool evening breeze blows across Mariko's face.

She listens to her mother howling at the moon. Tomiko howls three times as she circles Mariko. Mariko is too tired to ask her what she is doing.

Mariko lies down and goes to asleep.

When she awakens she can see the reflection of the moon on the water. She looks into the water and tumbles in. Mariko's arms flail. A sea turtle swoops under Mariko and guides her to the bottom of the pond.

"Where are you taking me?"

The sea turtle stops in front of a small castle.

"Welcome to my home, Mariko. My name is Umigame, Umi for short. Please come with me. I will teach you how to find your spirit animal from within."

Mariko follows Umi into the castle.

"I can't believe I can breathe and talk under water."

"Remember, anything is possible, Mariko. We are going to the other side of the castle through the back door. Once through the door it will take us to the *Meadow of Spirit Animals.*"

Umi stands in front of a ten-foot door. The bright red wooden door opens at his touch.

CHAPTER 6

Mariko walks through the door. She steps into a green meadow. There is an array of pink, red, and purple colored wild flowers and animals everywhere. The wind blows through Umi's long white hair and beard. His jade green eyes sparkle in the sunlight.

"Umi, where are you?" Mariko asks.

"I am here next to you, Mariko."

Umi takes her hand and reassures her.

"You are not a sea turtle anymore?"

"No, I am an old man. I am the Master Guide of the *Meadow of Spirit Animals.*"

Umi stares into Mariko's eyes.

"Let's take a walk through the meadow. You will meet five animals. Your spirit animal from within will be among them. Each will come and kiss your spirit eye."

"What is my spirit eye, Umi?

"It is the spot between your eyes. It's the third eye that you can't see but still exists in you. It takes you to the inner realms and to your higher consciousness. It's your spiritual self. There will be an animal that represents your true nature; this is your spirit animal from within. The others are your animal guides," Umi tells her.

Mariko feels something nudging her back. She turns and a fawn leaps up and kisses her spirit eye. Mariko wraps her arms around the fawn's neck and holds her close.

"I am Shika. I am your animal guide of the South; I represent the physical you," the fawn says.

"What do you mean by the 'physical you?'" Mariko asks.

"It's the part of you that is like a fawn. Fawns are tiny, delicate, gentle, and loving–just like you."

A black wolf slowly trots up to Mariko. The wolf's bright yellow eyes look deeply into her. She approaches Mariko and kisses her spirit eye.

"I am Okami. I am your animal guide of the West; I represent the emotional you."

"What does that mean?" Mariko asks.

"Wolves are loving, nurturing, and healing. They are also good teachers like you will be one day," Okami says.

A grey dolphin jumps out of the water and kisses Mariko's spirit eye. His skin is smooth to Mariko's touch.

"I am Iruka. I am your animal guide of the North; I represent the spiritual you. The part of you that is wild and free. You are a gatekeeper of other realms and like to live in harmony with others."

Mariko tries to understand and soak in all the information she is learning from her spirit guides. Her mind feels like it's twirling in mid-air. She wonders how she will remember all this.

A red fox circles Mariko several times and then kisses her spirit eye. His red fur is soft against her skin.

"I am Kitsune. I am your animal guide of the East; I represent the mental you. The you that is able to see the unseen, can fit in anywhere, and is very intelligent."

Kitsune winks at Mariko.

"Don't worry. You will remember everything," Umi says.

Mariko looks up towards the turquoise sky. A white butterfly flies up and sits on the tip of Mariko's nose. She giggles. The butterfly flutters away and sits on a flower petal nearby.

She doesn't kiss Mariko's spirit eye.

"It's time for you to leave now," Umi says.

He guides Mariko back to the large rock and kisses Mariko's spirit eye and disappears into the darkness.

"Wait, Umi, only four animals kissed my spirit eye. The white butterfly flew away."

Mariko looks around for Umi. He's gone.

CHAPTER 7

The morning sun beams down through the trees. Mariko lies on top of the large rock. She opens her eyes to see her mother sitting next to her.

"Mariko, did you see your spirit animal from within?" her mother asks.

"No, I didn't find my spirit animal. But I did find my animal guides. I thought my spirit animal was going to be the white butterfly but she looked at me and flew away. I told Umi what happened but he just kissed me and brought me back here."

"You say that Umi kissed you? Did he kiss your spirit eye? What animal was Umi when you met him?"

"He was a green sea turtle when he pulled me down into the water. When he brought me back his shell was an iridescent blue like moonstones. Umi kissed my spirit eye. I think my spirit animal is an iridescent blue sea turtle, Mommy."

"Yes. I watched you playing for hours in the water."

"Why do I still look like myself?"

"You are seeing your reflection of what you remembered from being on Earth. The next time you come you will be an iridescent blue sea turtle. You need to open yourself to new possibilities."

CHAPTER 8

"Mommy, can Daddy come and visit you here?"

"No, Mariko. You hold the magic in your heart. It's time for me to go. Next time we visit you can come as your spirit animal from within: an iridescent blue sea turtle."

"I will miss you, Mommy."

Tears fill Mariko's eyes.

"I will miss you too. Niji will always meet you at the Rainbow Bridge to guide you. Just look into the mirror and think of me. I will meet you in Rainbow Valley. I love you."

"I love you too, Mommy."

Tomiko nudges her daughter's face. Mariko gives her mother a big hug. She wakes up on her favorite rock in the tea garden. Mariko looks into the mirror and sees a reflection of herself.

Mariko wonders if she is dreaming.

A white owl appears on the old maple tree above her.

"No, Mariko. You were not dreaming," Niji says.

Memories of Rainbow Valley overwhelms Mariko's mind. She pulls out her pink leather journal and writes about her adventure. With the last stroke of her pen, the blue and pink horizon penetrates her soul and reminds her of her mother. She writes, "I love you, Mommy, and I'm not afraid anymore. I know you are watching over me. Thank you."

The End

ACKNOWLEDGEMENTS

I'd like to thank my husband Chris for his love, support, patience, and encouragement. Thank you for giving me the confidence to reach my dreams.

I'd like to thank my illustrator, Eko Setiawan for his beautiful artistry, diligence, professionalism, kindness, and patience throughout the illustration process.
http://facebook.com/kyozeshirou

Ramy Vance – Thank you for giving me the inspiration and motivation to write. You are an awesome writing coach. Ramy is the author of *Gonegod World* and other titles.
paradise-lot.com

Tasche Laine – Thank you for being the best accountability partner and friend ever. She is the author of *Closure* and *Chameleon.* http://taschelaine.com

Joan Seko – Thank you for your guidance and support. Joan is the author of *Lady Dahlia's Story.*

Tamara Fowler – Thank you for your positivity and help.
https://editkitten.com

Arlene Tognetti – Thank you for being a great motivator and friend. Arlene is the co-author of *The Complete Idiot's Guide to Tarot, 2nd Edition* and other books.

https://www.facebook.com/Mellinettis-201560279854152

Lynn Andrews – Thank you for your great teachings on shamanism, dreaming, and guiding me to believe in myself. Lynn has authored *Medicine Woman Series* and other books.

http://lynnandrews.com

Robert Moss –Thank you for your awesome teachings in dreaming and being aware of the multidimensional worlds. Robert is the author of *Conscious Dreaming* and other books on dreaming.

http://mossdreams.com

Made in the USA
Monee, IL
18 February 2020